단
순단하게
단아하게
게 SIMPLY,
FIRMLY,
GRACEFULLY

박노해 사진에세이

02

단순하게
단아하게

SIMPLY,
FIRMLY,
GRACEFULLY

PARK NOHAE PHOTO ESSAY 02

느린걸음

단순하게 단단하게 단아하게

Simply, Firmly, Gracefully

CONTENTS

The More
I Advance

Looking back,
I walked ahead,
walked toward you.

My hope is in what is simple,
my trust is in what is firm,
my love is for what is graceful.

Thus it was when I looked back.

Poverty made me simple,
suffering made me firm,
solitude made me graceful.

Such things could not kill me.
What could not kill me
made me greener.

The more I advance, the more I live.

Simply.
Firmly.
Gracefully.

가면 갈수록

뒤를 돌아보면서
앞을 향해 걸었다
너를 향해 걸었다

내 희망은 단순한 것
내 믿음은 단단한 것
내 사랑은 단아한 것

돌아보면 그랬다

가난이 나를 단순하게 만들었다
고난이 나를 단단하게 만들었다
고독이 나를 단아하게 만들었다

그것들은 나를 죽이지 못했다
나를 죽이지 못한 것들은
나를 더 푸르게 하였다

가면 갈수록 나 살아있다

단순하게
단단하게
단아하게

산 정 의 단 단 한 집

빛나는 만년설산을 가장 많이 품고 있지만
외부의 침략과 분쟁이 끊이지 않는 곳,
'국경의 운명'을 피할 수 없는 나라 파키스탄.
더는 지킬 수 없고 물러날 수 없는 날엔
만년설산에 싸인 저 단단한 암벽 산정으로
아이들과 노인과 여인들을 대피시켜왔다.
칠흑 같은 어둠 속 산정 희미한 불빛을 바라보며
저 불빛 하나만은 꺼뜨리지 않겠노라,
청년들은 다시 일어나 싸우며 이 땅을 지켜왔다.
모든 것이 무너져도 저 높은 곳의 사랑이 있는 한
결코 무릎 꿇릴 수 없는 것이 인간이기에.

❧

A SOLID HOUSE ON A MOUNTAINTOP

Pakistan, a land that can never escape its 'frontier destiny,' where external
aggressions and conflicts never cease, despite harboring the largest number
of bright snow-covered peaks. On days when neither defence nor retreat
were possible, children, old folk and women would be evacuated to the top
of that solid rock face girt round with snowy mountains. Gazing in pitch-
darkness at the peak's dim light, determined that its one light would not be
extinguished, young men rose up again, fought to defend their land. Though
everything crumbles, since there is love for that lofty spot, being human
means never being brought to one's knees.

Hunza, Northern Areas, Pakistan, 2011.

HIMALAYAN MORNING PRAYER

Trees bow white under the frost that fell all night, as morning in the Himalayan highlands awakens in blue light. After sweeping the yard that shines bright at daybreak they warm chilled bodies with sweet chai, then pray. Today may faces shine bright like the sun, may hearts be ennobled like the Himalayas, and may we greet good people. So morning comes, morning comes walking again, and once the sun has risen, we will live on.

Islamabad, Pakistan, 2011.

히말라야의 아침 기도

밤새 내린 서리로 하얗게 웅크렸던 나무들이
푸른 빛으로 깨어나는 히말라야 고원의 아침.
여명이 빛나는 흙마당을 깨끗이 쓸고
달콤한 짜이로 몸을 녹이며 기도를 바친다.
오늘도 해처럼 밝은 얼굴이기를.
히말라야처럼 고결한 마음이기를.
그리하여 좋은 이를 맞이하기를.
그렇게 아침이 오고, 또 아침이 걸어오고,
태양만 떠오르면 우리는 살아갈 테니.

호 수 같 은 마 음 으 로

만년설이 녹아 흐르는 호숫가에서
여인들은 빨래를 하며 명랑한 이야기를 나누고
뛰어놀던 아이들은 맑은 호숫물로 목을 축인다.
따끈히 달구어진 바위 위에 널어놓은 빨래에서
잘 마른 햇빛 내음이 솔솔 풍겨오면
호수 같은 마음을 품고 집으로 돌아간다.

❧

WITH HEARTS LIKE A LAKE

At the lakeside where the snowcaps melt and flow, women chatter merrily as they do the laundry while children quench their thirst with the clear water after playing. Once a well-dried smell of sunshine rises gently from the laundry spread on sun-warmed rocks they head for home with hearts like the lake.

Gupis, Northern Areas, Pakistan, 2011.

누비아 사막의 농부

사막을 달구던 태양이 저물어가면
흰 잘라비를 입은 수단의 농부들은
나일 강물을 끌어다 이랑을 내고 씨앗을 뿌린다.
거대한 모래폭풍이 한번 휩쓸고 지나가면
그동안의 노고는 흔적도 없이 사라지지만,
말라 죽으면 다시 심고 또 말라 죽으면
다시 심는 일을 원망도 불평도 없이 해나간다.
그렇게 한 걸음 한 걸음씩 나일강 주변으로
'푸른 띠'를 이루며 넓어지는 농토와 숲.
날마다 반복되는 농부들의 성사聖事 덕분에
오늘도 불타는 사막에 푸른 생명이 자라난다.
나는 걸음마다 황무지를 늘려가는 사람인가.
걸음마다 푸른 지경地境을 넓혀가는 사람인가.

⚘

A NUBIAN DESERT FARMER

When the sun that has been heating the desert disappears, Sudanese farmers dressed in white jellabiyas draw up water from the Nile, dig furrows, sow seeds. If ever a huge sandstorm comes sweeping through, all their hard work disappears without trace, but if a crop dries up and dies, they plant it again, and if it dries up again they set about planting again, no resentment, no complaining. So, step by step, farmland and forest form and make wider a 'green belt' along the Nile. Thanks to the farmers' sacred work, repeated day after day, today, still, green life grows up from the scorching desert. Am I one who with every step expands the wilderness? Am I one who with every step expands the boundaries of green land?

Old Dongola, Nubian, Sudan, 2008.

FLOWERING LABOR

Kyun Myaw, farms floating on the waters of Inle Lake. The heart of this vast farm is a flower garden offered up in a shrine. In Burma, even poor families devote one tenth of their income to buying flowers every morning to offer at a Buddhist shrine, and pray. It's as if, though eating is important, life is more a matter of flowers than rice. Ma Moe Sheh, harvesting flowers in a tiny boat, says: "In this little patch of land rocking on the water flowers bloom each in their own colors and give off their scent. I find myself smiling at the scent, even when working hard. I hope that I can give off a sweet scent with my flowery smile, whether times are good or bad."

Lake Inle, Nyaung Shwe, Burma, 2011.

꽃 피는 노동

인레 호수의 '물 위에 떠 있는 농장' 쭌묘.
이 광대한 쭌묘의 심장은 불전에 오르는 꽃밭이다.
버마에서는 가난한 집안도 소득의 1/10을 바쳐
매일 아침 꽃을 사 불전에 올리며 기도를 한다.
먹고 사는 일이 중요해도 삶은, 밥보다 꽃이라는 듯이.
조각배를 타고 꽃을 수확하는 마 모에 쉐.
"물 위에 흔들리는 이 한 뼘의 땅에서도
꽃은 제 빛깔로 피어나고 향기를 내요.
고된 노동 속에서도 그 향기에 미소 짓게 돼요.
저도 좋은 때나 힘든 때나 꽃다운 미소로
향기를 주는 사람이면 좋겠어요."

연꽃 줄기로 옷감을 짜는 여인

인레 호수에 연꽃이 핀 풍경은 아름답기 그지없다.
ㄴ 연꽃 줄기에서 실을 뽑는 연사蓮絲 생산 또한 유명하다.
연분홍색 연꽃에서만 채취할 수 있어 양이 많지 않고,
마보다도 시원하고 비단처럼 부드러워 고가에 나간다.
소녀 때부터 40년 넘게 전통 옷감을 짜온 여인에게서
'물질의 심장'을 꽃피우는 장인의 기품이 어려 나온다.

❧

A WOMAN WEAVING CLOTH
USING LOTUS STALKS

The sight of lotus flowers blossoming on Inle Lake is immensely beautiful.
It is also famous for the production of yarn using thread made from lotus
stalks. It only uses the stems of pale pink lotus flowers, so there is not much
of it, and as it is cooler than hemp, soft like silk, it sells for a high price.
A woman who has been weaving traditional cloth for more than forty years,
ever since she was a young girl, displays the elegance of a craftsman who
brings to blossom the "heart of a substance."

Lake Inle, Nyaung Shwe, Burma, 2011.

연자방아로 땅콩기름을 짜다

키 큰 탐빈나무 사이로 노을이 물드는 시간.
물소가 버마의 전통 연자방아 '씨 쩨익 송'을
느릿느릿 돌리며 고소한 땅콩기름을 짜고 있다.
연자방아는 인류의 가장 오래된 기구 중 하나로
더 이상 덧붙일 것도 덜어낼 것도 없는 도구다.
최고의 삶의 기술은 언제나 가장 단순한 것으로
가장 풍요로운 삶을 꽃피우는 것이 아닌가.

℘

AN OX-MILL PRESSING PEANUT OIL

The hour when the setting sun shines between tall palm trees. The water buffalo is slowly turning the traditional Burmese mill 'Si kyate sone' used to press savory peanut oil. The ox-mill is one of mankind's oldest implements, one that needs nothing to be added or taken away. Surely, life's finest skills, being always the simplest, bring life of plenty to bloom?

Nyaung-U, Bagan, Burma, 2011.

FLOWERBEDS BUILT ON MUD

The village of Dala, across the river from Yangon, the major city of Burma, is the last shelter for poor people who can't afford expensive homes after being driven out and driven away. No electricity, no water supply, refugees after flooding, they receive almost no help from the government. But even amidst the worst poverty the people in Dala plant lotus and water hyacinths to purify the mud, build their houses, weaving bamboos with their own hands. The woman dressed in clean clothes who served me rice noodles sends me off with a smile like a flower, her graceful figure seeming to ask: Should I live thoughtlessly because life is hard? Could I allow poverty and misfortune to cloud my heart?

Dala, Yangon, Burma, 2011.

진창 위의 꽃밭

버마의 대도시 양곤의 강 건너편 달라 마을은
비싼 집값을 감당할 수 없는 가난한 민초들이
밀리고 떠밀려 마지막으로 모여든 보금자리다.
전기도 없고 수도도 없고, 홍수가 나 피난민이 되어도
정부로부터 거의 아무런 도움도 받지 못한다.
하지만 달라 마을 사람들은 최악의 가난 속에서도
진창을 정화해줄 연꽃과 부레옥잠을 심어 기르고
손수 대나무를 엮어 자신만의 집을 지어 살아왔다.
깨끗이 빤 옷차림으로 쌀국수를 대접해주는 여인은
생활이 고달프다 하여 함부로 살아가면 되겠냐는 듯,
가난과 불운이 마음까지 흐리게 해서야 되겠냐는 듯,
단아한 자태로 꽃 같은 미소를 지어 보낸다.

'올드 바자르'의 향신료 가게

'파키스탄의 심장'이라 불리는 비옥한 곡창지대 라호르에는
'없는 것만 빼고 다 있다'는 올드 바자르Old Bazaar가 있다.
말린 과일과 견과류, 양념과 약재로 쓰이는 수십 종의
향신료를 정갈하게 담아두고 손님을 맞이하는 상인.
그 옛날 라호르의 상인들은 실크로드를 통해
향신료를 수출하며 세계 역사를 뒤흔들었다.
그 향기와 기운은 오늘도 고풍 어린 골목마다 흐르고 있다.
무굴제국의 영광과 역사의 광채가 살아있는 올드 바자르의
상인들은 서구 자본의 뉴타운 건설에 맞서 이곳을 지켜간다.

❧

SPICE SHOPS IN THE OLD BAZAAR

In the fertile granary of Lahore, known as the "Heart of Pakistan," there is the
Old Bazaar, of which it is said, "It has everything but what it lacks." A merchant
welcomes customers with a neatly arranged stock of dried fruits, nuts and
dozens of kinds of spices used as seasoning and medicine. In the old days, Lahore
merchants traveled the Silk Road, exporting spices and influencing world history.
Today fragrance and energy go flowing down every ancient alley. The merchants
of the Old Bazaar, where the glory and brilliant history of the Mughal Empire
live on, protect this place from the building of a new town with western capital.

Lahore, Punjab, Pakistan, 2011.

DAZZLING FLAGS OF LIFE

For me, the laundry that flutters silently everywhere in the world is a flag
of peace brighter than any national flag. It urges us to wash away the sweat
of honest labor, to wash away the bloodstains of fierce bombing, to wash
away even the stains of weary hearts, though the clothes may be old and the
body tired, to clean and restore them, to keep advancing with steps filled
with new hope. Laundry bright with a strong will and a fighting spirit of
love. Laundry flapping, the most beautiful flags in the world.

Omdurman, Sudan, 2008.

눈부신 삶의 깃발

지상의 어디서나 소리 없이 나부끼는 빨래는
내겐 어떤 국기보다 빛나는 평화의 깃발이다.
정직한 노동의 땀방울을 씻어내고
사나운 폭격의 핏방울을 씻어내고
고단한 마음의 얼룩까지 씻어내고
비록 낡은 옷 지친 몸이지만 깨끗이 소생시켜
새 희망의 걸음으로 앞을 향해 나아가라 한다.
강인한 의지와 사랑의 투혼으로 빛나는 빨래들.
지상의 가장 아름다운 깃발로 펄럭이는 빨래들.

나귀야 조심조심

힌두쿠시 산맥의 굽이굽이 좁고 가파른 길에서
당나귀가 미끄러질까 봐 꼬리를 잡아주는 노인.
"이 나귀들은 나면서부터 나와 함께 걸었다오.
매일같이 산에서 나무를 지고 오고
수확한 곡물을 싣고 시장에 나가고,
딸아이 결혼식 날엔 요놈 등에 태워 시집 보내고
첫 손주를 낳았을 땐 따뜻한 이불을 실어 보냈지.
독립운동하는 청년들이 있는 저 산정으로
겨울 식량과 물자도 몰래 나르곤 했다오.
너무 무거운 짐을 얹어온 것 같아 미안하면서도
한평생 묵묵히 함께해준 것이 어찌나 고마운지…."
너희가 받쳐준 덕분에 이 삶의 무게를 지고 간다고,
생의 마지막 날까지 우리 할 일을 해나가자고,
험한 길마다 나귀야 조심조심 함께 걸어간다.

ॐ

DONKEY, BE CAREFUL

On a steep, narrow, winding path in the hills of the Hindu Kush an old man holds onto his donkey's tail for fear it might slip. "These donkeys have been walking with me since they were born. They bring wood down from the mountains day after day, take harvested grain to market, on my daughter's wedding day, I sent her off on the back of one, and when my first grandchild was born, I sent one carrying a warm blanket. They used secretly to take winter food and supplies up that mountain to the youths engaged in the independence movement. I feel sorry for so overloading them and more than grateful for their having been silently with us for a whole lifetime." He can bear life's burdens because of their support, he says, so will keep on doing what has to be done until life's last day, walking carefully together along every rough path.

Bumburet, Khyber Pakhtunkhwa, Pakistan, 2011.

파 슈 툰 의 목 자

미군의 무인폭격기가 차가운 폭음을 올리는 파슈툰에서
아직 잘 걷지 못하는 어린 양을 품에 안은 목자를 만났다.
"전쟁의 현실은 제가 어찌할 수 없지만
이 어린 양들은 제가 지켜줄 겁니다.
대대로 살아온 터전을 아이들에게 물려주고
어린 양의 울음소리가 그치지 않게 하는 것이
제가 이 생에 할 수 있는 최선의 일이겠지요."
생을 두고 끝까지 밀어 가는 사랑보다 강한 힘은 없으니.

꽃

SHEPHERD OF PASHTUN

In Pashtun where unmanned U.S. bombers produce harsh explosions I met a
shepherd hugging a lamb that was still not able to walk properly. "I can't do
anything about the reality of war but I'll protect these baby lambs. Passing on to
our children the land where we have lived for generations and ensuring that the
bleating of baby lambs never stops is the best thing I can do in this life." There
is no stronger force than the love that keeps forging ahead for a whole lifetime.

Dir, Khyber Pakhtunkhwa, Pakistan, 2011.

포도나무 아래서

만년설산에 둘러싸인 장쾌한 풍광의 파슈툰 마을.
할아버지는 자신의 할아버지가 심어 물려준
달콤한 포도나무 그늘로 어린 손주들을 부른다.
아이들은 작은 사슴처럼 귀를 쫑긋 세운 채
할아버지가 들려주는 재미난 이야기에 빠져든다.
오래된 꿈과 전설과 선조들의 영웅담,
온몸으로 겪어내온 좋고 나쁜 경험들,
자신을 더 나은 존재로 이끈 모험과 고난의 이야기는
아이들의 가슴에 강물처럼 흘러 비옥한 영토가 된다.
삶은, 자신만의 이야기를 남겨주는 것이다.
삶은, 이야기를 유산으로 물려주는 것이다.
그 삶의 이야기가 후대의 가슴속에 살아있는 한
그는 사랑했던 이들 곁에 영원히 살아있는 것이다.

❧

BENEATH A VINE

Pashtun Village is a thrilling sight, surrounded by snowy peaks. A grandfather
calls his little grandchildren into the sweet shade of a vine that he says was planted
and bequeathed by his own grandfather. The children prick up their ears like
small deer, absorbed in the funny stories told by their grandfather. Old dreams,
legends and heroic tales of ancestors, good and bad experiences he has undergone
himself, stories of the adventures and hardship that have made him a better
person, flow like a river into the hearts of the children that become fertile ground.
Life is about leaving behind your own unique story. Life is about bequeathing
stories as your inheritance. As long as the story of someone's life lives on in the
hearts of future generations they are forever alive beside those whom they loved.

Drosh, Khyber Pakhtunkhwa, Pakistan, 2011.

DOZING IN THE SHADE OF A TREE

After finishing the morning's work, gathering, sitting down to have lunch, it's time for a nap in the shade of a tree. A breeze blows bearing the breath of the distant sprouting wheat, the bed in the sunny yard is fresh. As the sunshine comes falling vertically and desire stretches out horizontally, it's perfect for a sweet nap. Just a moment in the shade of this green tree, before waking up and setting out again with strength restored.

Dohak Baba Fakheer village, Punjab, Pakistan, 2011.

나무 그늘 아래 낮잠

아침 노동을 마치고 모여 앉아 점심을 먹고 나면
자, 나무 그늘 아래서 낮잠에 들 시간이다.
저 멀리 밀싹의 숨결을 담은 바람이 불어오고
흙마당 맑은 햇살에 말린 침대는 찹찹하다.
태양이 수직으로 내리쬐고
욕망은 수평으로 뻗어갈 때,
여기서는 달콤한 낮잠에 빠져든다.
이 푸른 나무 그늘 아래 잠깐,
멈춰 선 힘으로 다시 깨어 나아갈 수 있도록.

꽃을 타고 온 아이

브로모 화산의 하얀 숨결에 아침 이슬이 빛날 때
할머니는 손주를 안고 집 앞 고원길을 산책한다.
'꽃을 타고 여기 온 아가야, 단아한 꽃처럼 자라거라.'
노래인 듯 기도인 듯 가만가만 속삭이는 소리에
꽃들도 향기를 날리며 아이를 향해 고개를 숙인다.
우리 모두는 꽃을 타고 온 아이.
비와 바람과 별과 태양이 길러준 대지의 선물과
앞서간 이들이 물려준 노동과 사랑의 꽃내림으로
이 지구별을 여행하다 저 하늘로 돌아가는 것이니.
꽃을 타고 온 아이야, 꽃처럼 피어나고 꽃처럼 빛나거라.

୬

A CHILD WHO CAME BY A FLOWER

When morning dew shines on the white breath of volcanic Mount Bromo,
grandma walks along the highland path in front of her house, holding her
grandchild. "Baby, you came by a flower, so now you must grow like a graceful
flower," in a quiet whisper, half song, half prayer, while the flowers give off
their scent and bow their heads toward the child. We are all children who
came by flowers, gifts of the ground raised by rain, wind, stars, and sun,
a flowering of the labors and love of those who have gone before, going back
to heaven after a trip to this earthly star. Baby, you came by a flower, bloom
like a flower, shine like a flower.

Probolinggo, East Java, Indonesia, 2013.

만 년 설 물 을 긷 다

깊은 산맥에 비밀스레 숨겨진 가쿠치 마을 사람들은
만년설이 녹아 흐른 물을 길어다 살아간다.
고독한 히말라야가 흘려보낸 맑은 눈물은
따뜻한 차가 되고 빵이 되고 여인의 미소로 피어난다.
만년설산 높고 시린 산정에선 아무도 살 수가 없지만
그것이 사라지면 이 대지에선 누구도 살 수가 없으니.
나는 신성한 빛으로 묵연히 서 있는 만년설산을 경외했네.
시련은 내가 받고 평온은 네게 주는 헌신의 존재를 사랑했네.

❧

DRAWING WATER FROM
PERPETUAL SNOW

The people of Gaguch, a village secretly hidden deep amidst mountains,
depend on the water flowing down when the snow melts. The clear
tears shed by the lonely Himalayas become hot tea, bread, bloom with a
woman's smile. Though no one can live at the very top of the snow-covered
mountains, if they disappears no one can live in this land. I venerated the
snowy mountains, as they stood silent in sacred light. I loved the existence of
the devotion that meant accepting trials for oneself and giving you peace.

Barsat village, Gaguch, Pakistan, 2011.

MOM'S COFFEE

Produced in the highlands of Sumatra 'Aceh Gayo Mountain Coffee' is one of the best coffees in the world. A family of coffee farmers who have kept the wild Liar traditional farming methods is sitting in a flowering yard waiting for 'mom's coffee.' After peeling the red coffee cherries that were selected individually then picked by hand, the light yellow coffee beans are washed in water and dried in the sun, then placed on an iron plate and roasted over a wood fire before being ground in a log grinder worn smooth with age. At the smell of the first coffee harvested this year, the children's hearts are already throbbing. In a simple life, the most peaceful and fullfilling moment on earth, is a sweet moment, enjoying a chat with your loved ones over a cup of coffee.

Takengon, Central Aceh, Sumatra, Indonesia, 2013.

엄마의 커피

수마트라섬의 고산지대에서 생산되는
'아체 가요 마운틴 커피'는 세계 최고의 커피로 손꼽힌다.
야생의 리아르Liar 전통 농법을 지켜온 커피 농부 가족이
꽃이 핀 마당에 모여 앉아 '엄마의 커피'를 기다린다.
손으로 일일이 골라 딴 빨간 커피 체리의 껍질을 벗긴 후
연노랑 빛 커피 콩을 물에 씻어 햇살에 말리고
무쇠판 위에 올려 장작불로 볶은 다음,
반질반질 닳은 오래된 '통나무 그라인더'로 빻는다.
올해 첫 수확한 커피 향기에 벌써 가슴이 콩닥이는 아이들.
간소한 생활 속에 이 지상의 가장 평온하고 충만한 시간,
사랑하는 이와 커피 한 잔의 담소를 누리는 그윽한 시간.

광야의 환대

아름드리 올리브나무가 끝없이 펼쳐진 광야 마을.
광야의 사람들은 침략자들에게는 결사항전하지만
길손은 누구라도 불러들여 따뜻이 환대한다.
온 가족이 웃음 지며 달콤한 샤이를 내오고
갓 구운 빵과 직접 기른 올리브를 대접한다.
"제 사랑하는 딸들에게 늘 말하곤 하지요.
문을 두드리는 낯선 이는 너의 길을 밝혀주기 위해
멀리서 찾아온 안내자이고 신이 보낸 이라고요."
세상은 사람과 사람이 만나는 곳이고
우리 삶은 속셈 없는 마음과 마음이 빚어가는 것.

❧

WILDERNESS HOSPITALITY

A desert village with huge olive trees stretching endlessly. The people of the desert resist invaders desperately, but they welcome any traveler, offering warm hospitality. The whole family smilingly brings out sweet chai, serves freshly baked bread and olives from their own trees. "I always tell my darling daughters that any stranger knocking on the door is a guide come from afar, one sent by God to lighten their path." The world is a place where people meet, our lives are realized by the union of hearts devoid of ulterior motives.

Jerash, Jordan, 2008.

세상에서 제일 높은 학교

지구의 등뼈인 안데스 고원 5천 미터 높이에
잉카의 후예인 께로족이 5백 년째 살고 있다.
께로스 주민들은 대대로 아이들에게 물려줄
세계에서 가장 높고 작은 학교를 지었다.
엄마가 알파카 털로 짜준 전통 옷을 차려입고
새벽부터 두세 시간을 걸어 학교에 온 아이들이
친구를 보자마자 빨갛게 언 볼로 신나게 뛰논다.
고원이 단련해준 강인한 심장으로
고독이 선물해준 천진한 웃음으로
결핍이 꽃피워준 단단한 우정으로
세계에서 제일 높고 작은 학교에서
세상에서 제일 크고 환한 웃음소리가 울린다.

❧

THE HIGHEST SCHOOL IN THE WORLD

5,000 meters up in the high plateaus of the Andes, the world's backbone, the Incas' descendants, the Q'ero, have been living for 500 years. Q'ero villagers built the highest and smallest school in the world that they will pass on from generation to generation. Children who set out for school at dawn and walked two or three hours wearing traditional clothes woven with alpaca fur by their mothers, the moment they spot their friends start to play with cheeks frozen red. With strong hearts trained by the plateau, with innocent smiles, gifts of loneliness, with firm friendship brought to blossom by lack, in the world's highest, smallest school, the loudest and brightest laughter in the world rings out.

Cochamuco, Cusco, Peru, 2010.

CHILDREN OF THE WIND

In the Andes where the air is thin at 4,000 meters above sea level children
go running, their bodies beating against the wind from the perpetual snows.
They have no toys yet they never stop laughing. After harvesting potatoes
from a sloping field mom and dad light a fire, bake the potatoes, and call from
afar. Truly, children, the world is full of dangers but you have the land of the
Andes, loving Pachamama, companions like starlight in the dark. Indeed, all
kinds of precious seeds are already planted in you so preserve them, endure,
hold each other's hands. Keep going along your way, be good and strong.

Patacancha, Cusco, Peru, 2010.

바람의 아이들

공기도 희박한 해발 4천 미터 안데스 고원에서
온몸으로 만년설 바람을 맞으며 달리는 아이들.
아무런 장난감이 없어도 웃음소리가 끝이 없다.
비탈진 밭에서 감자를 수확하던 엄마 아빠가
불을 지펴 감자를 구워 놓고 멀리서 부른다.
그래 아이야, 세계는 위험 가득한 곳이지만
너에겐 안데스의 대지와 자애로운 파차마마와
어둠 속의 별빛 같은 동무들이 있단다.
네 안에는 고귀한 씨알이 이미 다 심겨있으니
지켜내라, 견뎌내라, 서로 손을 잡아라.
착하고 강하게 너의 길을 가거라.

티 베 트 의 유 목 민

중국의 강제 점령에 맞서 저항해온 동티베트인들.
이 광대한 초원에 양과 야크 떼만 점점이 보일 뿐
가도 가도 막막한 지평에 구름과 바람만 고요히 흐른다.
멀리서 사람이 보이자 말을 타고 달려온 청년이
탁 트인 호감의 미소로 시원한 인사를 건넨다.
"짊어지고 살아갈 것이 적으니 마음은 편안하죠.
그래도 이 끝없는 초원에 나 홀로인 것 같아 적막해지고
달라이 라마를 생각하다 슬퍼질 때면 말을 타고 달려요.
가슴을 다 열고 초원의 빛과 하늘과 바람에 안기면
내 안의 우울이 다 살라지는 것 같거든요."

❧

NOMADS IN TIBET

East Tibetans have resisted the Chinese occupation. On these vast
grasslands, the only things visible are, here and there, flocks of sheep or yaks.
As you travel on, clouds and wind are the only things moving quietly over
the immense landscape. As soon as he glimpses someone in the distance, a
young man comes galloping on horseback and offers a friendly greeting with
a broad smile of goodwill. "My mind is at peace since I have few burdens
to carry. But I feel lonely, seeming to be the only person on these endless
grasslands and if I feel sad thinking about the Dalai Lama, I go galloping
away on horseback. When I open my heart wide and embrace the grasslands'
light and sky and wind the gloom inside me all seems to be sloughed off."

Ruoergai, Amdo Tibet, 2012.

AS THE SEASONS PASS

When the dry season begins in the Andes plateaus the soon-to-be-harvested quinoa, oats, alfalfa, barley, corn and taro shine, each with its own color and the land is colored like a picture. Andean farmers returning home with their flocks, a load of potatoes wrapped in a bundle, walk on among this great land's works of art, a combination of their labors and the sky's weather. They meditate on the seasons of their past life, the days lived as the seasons passed by, according to each season. Sprouting freshly green with the spring, blazing up as green flames with the summer, ripening, heads bowed, with the autumn, journeying on, shivering white, with the winter, but, ah, since I am a bearer of the fire of love how far has my heart traveled along the paths of eternity?

Misminay, Cusco, Andes, Peru, 2010.

계절이 지나가는 대로

안데스 고원에 건기가 시작되면
수확을 앞둔 끼누아와 귀리, 알팔파, 보리,
옥수수, 따루이가 저마다의 빛깔로 빛나며
대지는 한 폭의 그림처럼 물들어간다.
보자기에 감자알을 묵직이 담아 메고
양 떼를 몰고 귀가하는 안데스의 농부는
자신의 노동과 하늘의 기후가 함께 그려낸
이 위대한 대지의 작품 사이를 걸으며
지나온 생의 계절을 묵상한다.
계절이 지나가는 대로 계절 따라 살아온 날들.
봄과 함께 파릇파릇 돋아나고
여름과 함께 초록 불로 타오르고
가을과 함께 고개 숙여 익어가고
겨울과 함께 하얗게 떨며 걸어온 여정이지만
아, 나는 사랑의 불을 품고 운반하는 자이니
내 마음은 그 영원의 길을 얼마나 걸었던가.

안데스의 멋쟁이 농부

'신의 선물'이라 불리는 끼누아는 수천 년 동안
오직 저 높은 안데스 고원에서만 재배되어왔다.
한 해 동안 길러온 귀한 끼누아를 수확하는 날,
농부는 제일 아끼는 모자와 옷을 갖춰 입고서
잘 갈아 둔 낫으로 힘차게 거두어 간다.
탄탄한 두 발로 대지를 딛고 살아온 건강한 몸과
쉽게 좌절하지 않는 영혼을 가진 농부에게서
자신감에 찬 푸른 기운과 멋이 흘러나오는 듯하다.
남들이 준 자신감은 그들이 다시 가져갈 수 있지만
세상이 빼앗을 수 없는 자기만의 삶을 가진 사람은
어려움이 닥치고 시간이 흐를수록 더 굳건한 것이니.

❦

A GRACEFUL FARMER IN THE ANDES

For thousands of years quinoa, known as the "Gift of God," was only grown
on these high Andes plateaus. On the day the precious quinoa he has tended
for a year is to be harvested, the farmer puts on his best hat and clothes and
sets about harvesting it powerfully with a well-sharpened sickle. Green
energy and elegance full of self-confidence seem to flow from the farmer,
whose soul is not easily discouraged, healthy in body, treading the ground
with two firm feet. The confidence that others give may be taken back again,
but people who have their own lives that the world cannot take from them
only grow more steadfast the more difficulties come and time goes by.

Misminay, Cusco, Andes, Peru, 2010.

사탕수수밭의 소녀

키 큰 사탕수수 사이를 날래게 누비며
검무를 추듯 사탕수수를 수확하는 소녀.
이 거친 노동으로 1,500원 정도를 벌기에
장갑이 닳을까 헝겊을 손에 감고 일한다.
"'피부가 검어지면 루비 같은 사람이 되고
피부가 희어지면 잡석 같은 사람이 된다.'
제가 좋아하는 버마의 속담이에요.
사탕수수를 베어 달콤한 설탕을 짜내듯
나쁜 것들을 베며 제 꿈을 이뤄갈 거예요."
칼을 쥔 자는 두 부류다.
무도한 권력의 칼로 세상을 망치는 자와
살림의 칼을 쥐고 세상을 지키는 자.
정말로 그녀는 최고로 아름다운 칼잡이였다.

❧

A GIRL IN A SUGARCANE FIELD

Quickly making her way between tall sugar canes, a girl harvests the cane as
if performing a sword dance. Since she only earns about a dollar by this hard
labor, she works with cloth wrapped around her hands to protect her gloves.
"There's a Burmese saying I'm fond of: 'If your skin burns black, you grow
ruby-like, if your skin is white, you turn into rubble.' Just as sweet sugar is
pressed from the cut sugar cane, my dreams will come true as I cut away bad
things." There are two kinds of people who wield a sword: those who ruin the
world with the immoral sword of power, and those who protect the world with
the sword of housekeeping. She was truly the most beautiful swordswoman.

Nyaung Shwe, Burma, 2011.

탕 크 와 를 저 어 갈 때

청나일강이 발원하는 에티오피아 고원의
바다처럼 드넓은 타나 호수에서
파피루스로 엮은 전통 배 당크와를 탄 소년.
신발을 벗고 맨발로 물살을 느끼며
장대 하나로 균형을 잡아 나아가는
저 소년은 힘이 강한 것이 아니다.
자연의 리듬에 맞춰 그 흐름을 타고
자신을 조화시키는 힘을 익힌 것이다.
불필요한 동작과 장식과 소유를 다 덜어내고
최대한 단순하고, 단단하고, 단아하게 나아가는
소년의 몸짓에 만물의 정령이 깃들지 않는가.

ॐ

WHEN ROWING A TANKWA

A boy rows a traditional tankwa boat made of papyrus over Lake Tana, wide
as the sea, in the Ethiopian plateau where the Blue Nile rises. Taking off
his shoes, feeling the water with his bare feet, advancing balanced on one
pole, that boy is not someone strong. It's a matter of mastering the power to
harmonize himself, ride the flow, become one with the rhythms of nature.
Having cast off all unnecessary gestures, decorations, possessions, it's as
though the spirit of all things dwells in the boy's gestures as he advances as
simply as possible simply, firmly, gracefully.

Lake Tana, Bahir Dar, Ethiopia, 2008.

AT THE FRONTIER BETWEEN
TWO WORLDS

Once in a lifetime all Burma's boys become Buddhist monks for a while. After leaving their parents' home and shaving their heads, all they have is a robe and a bowl for food. They spend "mundane time" barefooted meeting simple folk, kneeling on the street every morning, receiving offerings of food, then they begin "monastic time," practicing alone in the temple. Standing at the door of the boundary between the two worlds, mundane and monastic, the voices of the boy monks reciting sutras ring clear: 'Seek light in yourself, seek light in the Dharma,' Take time to find the light in oneself, light the lamp of truth. The boys who treasure the mystery of this moment, the inwardness will live advancing as pilgrims between the two worlds.

Nyaung Shwe, Burma, 2011.

두 세 상 사 이 의 경 계 에 서

버마의 아이들은 일생에 한 번 단기 출가를 한다.
부모의 품을 떠나 머리를 깎고 나면
가진 건 가사 한 벌과 밥그릇 하나.
아침마다 길바닥에 무릎을 꿇고 밥을 공양하는
민초들을 맨발로 만나는 '속俗의 시간'을 걷고 나면,
사원에서 홀로 수행하는 '승僧의 시간'이 시작된다.
승과 속, 두 세상 사이 경계의 문에 서서
경전을 독송하는 동자승의 목소리가 낭랑하다.
'자등명 법등명自燈明 法燈明'
내 안의 빛을 밝혀 진리의 등불을 비추는 시간.
이 순간의 신비와 내면의 느낌을 간직한 아이들은
두 세상 사이 '순례자의 걸음'으로 살아가리라.

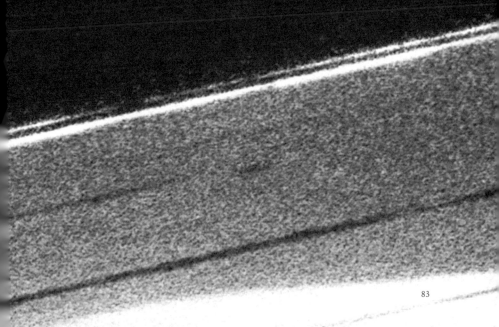

바 위 산 같 은 믿 음 으 로

분쟁의 긴장이 흐르는 국경 마을 카살라.
수민들은 하루 세 번 모스크에 모여서
간절한 기도를 바치고 포옹을 나눈다.
전쟁의 반대는 평화가 아니라
좋은 삶을 살아가는 일상이고
내가 먼저 좋은 사람이 되는 거라고,
바위산처럼 단단한 믿음으로
무릎을 꿇고 기도를 드린다.

❧

WITH FAITH LIKE A ROCK

Kassala, a frontier town where tensions and conflict run deep. The citizens
gather in the mosque three times each day, pray earnestly, then embrace.
The opposite of war is not peace, it's living a good life, each resolving to
become a good person first, with faith firm as rock, kneeling and praying.

Kassala, Sudan, 2008.

단 한 권 의 책

에티오피아 고원에 자리한 타나 호수 위에
400년 된 아름답고 경건한 수도원이 있다.
늙은 수도자는 1,500년 된 게에즈어 성서를
나직하고 깊은 음성으로 읽어 나간다.
"진실한 것은, 단 하나면 충분하지요.
난 단 한 권의 책을 날마다 읽고 묵상해왔지요.
읽을 때마다 처음 본 책처럼 새롭지요."
시간을 견뎌낸 단 하나의 오래된 것은
유행을 거슬러 언제나 새롭게 되살아난다.

❧

A SINGLE BOOK

Above Lake Tana on the Ethiopian plateau there is a beautiful, venerable monastery 400 years old. An old monk reads in a low, deep voice from a 1,500-year-old Ge'ez Bible. "Just one true thing is enough. I have ever read and meditated this one book each day. Every time I read it, it's as new as a book seen for the first time." A single old thing that has survived through time, against fashion, ever keeps being born anew.

Bahir Dar, Ethiopia, 2008.

작디작은 모스크

황량한 원시의 풍경이 끝없이 펼쳐지는
파키르 마을의 수백 년 된 흙벽돌 모스크.
세상에서 제일 작고 아름한 이 성전에서
아이들이 온몸에 햇살을 받으며 책을 읽는다.
이 모스크는 마을의 대소사를 치르는 장소이고
회의장이고 카페이고 기도처이기도 하다.
누구든 이용할 수 있고 모두가 함께 가꿔가는
공동체의 장소가 살아있다는 것은 얼마나 중요한가.
고향의 정자나무처럼, 샘터처럼, 동네 골목길처럼,
그 공용의 터전에는 함께하여 지혜롭고 다정하던
나누는 마음씨들이 살아있었으니.

❧

A TINY MOSQUE

A centuries-old mud-brick mosque in the village of Fakheer where the
desolate primitive landscape unfolds endlessly. In this shrine, the smallest
and most compact in the world, children are reading books, basking in the
sunshine. This mosque is the place for matters great and small, a meeting
hall, café, and a place of prayer. How important it is to have a place of
community alive that anyone can use, that all cultivate together. Like a home
village's shade tree, like a spring, like a neighborhood alley, gathered in such
shared public spaces, hearts wise and kind, ever sharing, once lived.

Dohak Baba Fakheer village, Punjab, Pakistan, 2011.

YET STILL THE CHILDREN LAUGH

The world's largest minority, the Kurds have lost their homeland. 35 million live scattered across Turkey, Iran, Iraq and Syria, aspiring to liberation amid oppression and discrimination. In the Zagros mountains, 4,000 meters above sea level, Kurdish sons and daughters resist, carrying 'soul guns' still today. Without news of sisters and brothers, who set off for the mountains in tears, in the shut-down school riddled with bullet marks, children still laugh. Having wept for too long, Kurdish children laugh. 'Neither darkness nor gunshots nor misfortune could kill me, and the things that could not kill me have become my strength.'

Hakkari, Kurdistan, Turkey, 2005.

그래도 아이들은 웃는다

나라 잃은 세계 최대의 소수민족 쿠르드.
3,500만 명이 터키, 이란, 이라크, 시리아 등에 흩어져
억압과 차별 속에 해방을 열망하며 살아간다.
해발 4천 미터 자그로스 산맥에는 오늘도
'영혼의 총'을 들고 저항하는 쿠르드의 아들딸이 있다.
산으로 울며 떠난 언니 오빠는 소식도 알 수 없지만
총탄 자국이 난 폐교에서, 그래도 아이들은 웃는다.
너무 오래 울어와서 쿠르드 아이들은 웃는다.
'어둠도 총성도 불운도 나를 죽이지 못했으니
나를 죽이지 못한 것들은 나의 힘이 되었으니.'

홍수가 쓸고 간 학교

마을에 큰 홍수가 있었다.

아직 다 복구하지 못한 학교에서

살아남은 아이들이 모여 수업을 한다.

무슨 사연일까, 자꾸만 문밖을 바라보는 소녀.

하루아침에 고아가 되고 만 걸까.

오지 못한 짝꿍을 떠올리는 걸까.

죽은 자들이 그립고 아파와도

소녀는 눈물을 삼키며 앞을 바라본다.

그저 고개 들어 앞을 바라보는 것이

필사적인 투쟁이 되는 사람들이 있다.

소녀가 한번 맑게 웃는다. 장하다. 고맙다.

돌아서는 나는 자꾸만 눈이 젖는다.

꽃

A SCHOOL SWEPT AWAY IN A FLOOD

There was a big flood in the village. In the school that has not yet been fully rebuilt the surviving children gather for classes. What's her story, that girl who keeps looking outside? Was she orphaned overnight? Is she recalling a deskmate? Though she's missing those who died, and hurting, she swallows her tears and looks ahead. There are people for whom just looking up and looking ahead represent a desperate struggle. The girl smiles brightly once. Great. Thank you. As I turn away, my eyes are moist.

Garut, West Java, Indonesia, 2013.

카슈미르의 저녁

분쟁의 땅 카슈미르에서 오늘도
총칼의 공기가 무겁게 감싸던 하루가 저문다.
엄마는 저녁 준비를 위해 불을 지피고
어린 딸은 식탁에 차릴 그릇을 꺼낸다.
창밖에는 히말라야의 눈보라가 날려도
장작불은 타오르고, 그래도 우리 함께 있으니,
이 작은 집에서 서로를 바라보며
불의 사랑으로 봄을 기다릴지니.
인간은, 세계 전체가 짓누르고 죽이려 해도
속마음을 나누고 이해하고 믿어주고 안아주는
단 한 평의 장소, 단 한 사람이 곁에 있다면,
그 사랑이면 살아지는 것이니.

❧

EVENING IN KASHMIR

Again today in Kashmir, disputed land, the sun is setting on one more day heavily shrouded in knives and guns. Mom lights the fire to cook dinner, the young daughter takes out the bowls to set the table. Even if there is a snowstorm in the Himalayas outside the window, still the fire is burning, and we're together, and as we look at each other in this little house we await spring with a fiery love. Even if the whole world tries to crush and kill human beings, so long as there's just one place, one person there beside you sharing, understanding, believing, embracing your inner heart, so long as that love is there, you're alive.

Wagnat village, Jammu Kashmir, India, 2013.

간절한 기도

이 마을의 신전은 수백 년 된 노거수다.
하루 일을 마치고 강물에 몸을 씻은 여인이
하얀 쌀가루로 정성껏 기도 문양을 그리고
귀한 기름을 부어 불을 켠 후 절을 올린다.
이 지상의 가장 낮은 계급의 가난한 여인이
자신의 가장 좋은 것을 바치며 기도를 드린다.
둥근 눈물방울 같은 몸으로 땅에 이마를 대고
간절하게, 간절하게, 기도를 드린다.

☙

A FERVENT PRAYER

This village's shrine is a centuries-old tree. A woman who has washed in
the river after the day's work carefully draws a mandala with white rice
flour, pours out precious oil, lights a lamp, bows to the ground. A poor
woman of the lowest caste on earth offers the best she has as she prays.
With a body like a rounded teardrop, she puts her forehead to the ground
and prays fervently, fervently.

Auli village, Orissa, India, 2013.

OLIVE TREE TEMPLE

More than 2,200 years ago, the world's first parchment, the first hospital, etc., the glorious ancient city of Pergamon, birthplace of many "firsts." Leaving behind those splendid times and hours of shame, too, the temples of the Acropolis have been ruined by the storms of time. But amidst all the ruins, all alone, a green vitality, I hear the words of the olive tree blowing in the wind. Before the winds of time sweeping everything away, what will fall, what survive? What will be forgotten and what remain green? In the light of history, ultimately, what is more important?

Bergama, Turkey, 2005.

올리브나무 신전

2,200여 년 전 세계 최초의 양피지, 최초의 병원 등
수많은 '최초'를 탄생시킨 영광의 고대 도시 페르가몬.
그 화려한 시대도 치욕의 시간도 뒤로 하고
아크로폴리스 신전들은 세월의 풍파에 소멸 중인데
폐허의 유적지에서 유일하게 푸른 생기로
바람에 날리는 올리브나무의 전언傳言을 듣는다.
모든 것을 쓸어가는 시간의 바람 앞에
무엇이 무너지고 무엇이 살아날까.
무엇이 잊혀지고 무엇이 푸르를까.
역사의 조망에 비추어 정녕, 무엇이 더 중요한가.

단 순 하 게 단 단 하 게 단 아 하 게

거대한 모래폭풍인 '하붑'이 지나가고
누비아 사막에 푸른 여명이 밝아오면
나일강에도 아침 태양이 떠오른다.
하지만 사막의 진정한 태양은 여인들이다.
단순한 살림으로 삶은 풍요롭고
단단한 내면으로 앞은 희망차고
단아한 기품으로 주위가 다 눈이 부신
사막의 아침 태양은 그녀들이다.
내 생의 모든 아침은 바로 그대이다.

❧

SIMPLY, FIRMLY, GRACEFULLY

After a huge sandstorm called a haboob has passed, day breaks in the Nubian
desert and the sun rises over the Nile. But the true sun in the desert is the
women. With simple living, life is abundant, with a firm inner self, the future
is hopeful, with their gracefulness, making everything around dazzling. The
desert's morning sun are those women. You are every morning of my life.

Old Dongola, Nubian, Sudan, 2008.

내 마음 깊은 곳의 방

안데스 산맥에 둘러싸인 고원 위에 서 있는
산타 카탈리나 봉쇄 수도원 Monastery of Santa Catalina.
1580년에 세워져 400여 년간 외부와 단절한 채
세상의 슬픔과 고통을 품고 '침묵의 불'로 타올라왔다.
열여덟에 여기 들어와 한평생 청빈과 노동과
침묵으로 기도를 바치다 선종한 수도자의 방.
필사적인 자기 소유와 자기 홍보의 시대에
지상의 높고 깊은 자리에 빛나는 한 평의 방.
지상에서 내가 이룬 업적들은 먼지처럼 흩어져도
아 나는 무력한 사랑의 마음 하나 바치며 이 길을 가네.

❧

A ROOM DEEP INSIDE MY HEART

Rising above a plateau surrounded by the Andes, the Monastery of Santa
Catalina. Built in 1580, cut off from the outside for over 400 years, embracing
the world's sorrows and suffering, it burned as "silent fire." The room of a
monk who entered at eighteen, spent a whole lifetime in honest poverty,
labor, praying in silence, then died. In a time of desperate possession and self-
promotion a tiny room shining in a high, deep place on earth. Even though
my achievements on earth scatter like dust, ah, I go my way, offering a heart
of powerless love.

Arequipa, Peru, 2010.

FROM THE PEAK OF MACHU PICCHU

Machu Picchu, the last Inca fortress and refuge, the only place untouched by the
Spanish invaders, has become the pride of the artists and revolutionaries of South
America. Concealed by the Andes jungle and the clouds of the mountaintops it
lay secretly hidden for many years. That firm, simple, graceful architecture,
a dandelion that bloomed tenaciously in a crack in a stone wall, the deep-set eyes
of children driving alpacas, declare; We're still alive here, We're standing up
again, making us contemplate the hidden meanings of history and humanity.

Machu Picchu, Cusco, Peru, 2010.

마추픽추 산정에서

잉카 최후의 요새이자 피난처였던 마추픽추는
스페인 침략자들에게 훼손되지 않은 유일한 곳으로
남미의 예술가와 혁명가들의 자부심이 된 곳이다.
안데스 산맥의 밀림과 산정의 구름에 가려져
오랜 세월 동안 비밀스레 숨겨져 있었다.
저 단단하고 단순하고 단아한 건축,
돌벽 틈에 끈질기게 피어난 민들레 한 송이,
알파카를 몰고 가는 아이들의 깊은 눈동자는
우린 아직 여기 살아있다고,
우린 다시 일어서고 있다고,
역사와 인간의 비의秘意를 묵상하게 한다.

전쟁의 레바논에서, 박노해. Park Nohae in the battlefield of Lebanon, 2007.

박노해

1957 전라남도에서 태어났다. 16세에 상경해 낮에는 노동자로 일하고 밤에는 선린상고(야간)를 다녔다. **1984** 27살에 첫 시집 『노동의 새벽』을 출간했다. 이 시집은 독재 정권의 금서 조치에도 100만 부 가까이 발간되며 한국 사회와 문단을 충격으로 뒤흔들었다. 감시를 피해 사용한 박노해라는 필명은 '박해받는 노동자 해방'이라는 뜻으로, 이때부터 '얼굴 없는 시인'으로 알려졌다. **1989** 〈남한사회주의노동자동맹〉(사노맹)을 결성했다. **1991** 7년여의 수배 끝에 안기부에 체포, 24일간의 고문 후 '반국가단체 수괴' 죄목으로 사형이 구형되고 무기징역에 처해졌다. **1993** 감옥 독방에서 두 번째 시집 『참된 시작』을 출간했다. **1997** 옥중에세이 『사람만이 희망이다』를 출간했다. **1998** 7년 6개월 만에 석방되었다. 이후 민주화운동 유공자로 복권됐으나 국가보상금을 거부했다. **2000** "과거를 팔아 오늘을 살지 않겠다"며 권력의 길을 뒤로 하고 비영리단체 〈나눔문화〉(www.nanum.com)를 설립했다. **2003** 이라크 전쟁터에 뛰어들면서, 전 세계 가난과 분쟁 현장에서 평화활동을 이어왔다. **2010** 낡은 흑백 필름 카메라로 기록해온 사진을 모아 첫 사진전 「라 광야」展과 「나 거기에 그들처럼」展(세종문화회관)을 열었다. 12년 만의 시집 『그러니 그대 사라지지 말아라』를 출간했다. **2012** 나눔문화가 운영하는 〈라 카페 갤러리〉에서 상설 사진전을 개최하고 있다. 현재 20번째 전시를 이어가고 있으며, 총 33만 명의 관람객이 다녀갔다. **2014** 아시아 사진전 「다른 길」展(세종문화회관) 개최와 함께 『다른 길』을 출간했다. **2019** 박노해 사진에세이 시리즈 『하루』, 『단순하게 단단하게 단아하게』, 『길』을 출간했다. **2020** 첫 번째 시 그림책 『푸른 빛의 소녀가』를 출간했다. **2021** 『걷는 독서』를 출간했다. 감옥에서부터 30년간 써온 한 권의 책, '우주에서의 인간의 길'을 담은 사상서를 집필 중이다. '적은 소유로 기품 있게' 살아가는 〈참사람의 숲〉을 꿈꾸며, 오늘도 시인의 작은 정원에서 꽃과 나무를 심고 기르며 새로운 혁명의 길로 나아가고 있다.

매일, 사진과 글로 시작하는 하루 〈박노해의 걷는 독서〉 ⓘ park_nohae Ⓕ parknohae

Park Nohae

Park Nohae is a legendary poet, photographer and revolutionary. He was born in 1957. While working as a laborer in his 20s, he began to reflect and write poems on the sufferings of the laboring class. He then took the pseudonym Park Nohae ("No" means "laborers," "Hae" means "liberation"). At the age of twenty-seven, Park published his first collection of poems, titled *The Dawn of Labor*, in 1984. Despite official bans, this collection sold nearly a million copies, and it shook Korean society with its shocking emotional power. Since then, he became an intensely symbolic figure of resistance, often called the "Faceless Poet." For several years the government authorities tried to arrest him in vain. He was finally arrested in 1991. After twenty-four days of investigation, with illegal torture, the death penalty was demanded for his radical ideology. He was finally sentenced to life imprisonment. After seven and a half years in prison, he was pardoned in 1998. Thereafter, he was reinstated as a contributor to the democratization movement, but he refused any state compensation. Park decided to leave the way for power, saying, "I will not live today by selling the past," and he established a nonprofit social movement organization "Nanum Munhwa," meaning "Culture of Sharing," (www.nanum.com) faced with the great challenges confronting global humanity. In 2003, right after the United States' invasion of Iraq, he flew to the field of war. Since then, he often visits countries that are suffering from war and poverty, such as Iraq, Palestine, Pakistan, Sudan, Tibet and Banda Aceh, in order to raise awareness about the situation through his photos and writings. He continues to hold photo exhibitions, and a total of 330,000 visitors have so far visited his exhibitions. He is writing a book of reflexions, the only such book he has written during the thirty years since prison, "The Human Path in Space." Dreaming of the Forest of True People, a life-community living "a graceful life with few possessions," the poet is still planting and growing flowers and trees in his small garden, advancing along the path toward a new revolution.

〈Park Nohae's Reading while Walking Along〉 ⓘ park_nohae ⓕ parknohae

저 서

Books

박노해 사진에세이 시리즈

01 하루
02 단순하게 단단하게 단아하게
03 길

박노해 시인이 20여 년 동안 지상의
멀고 높은 길을 걸으며 기록해온
'유랑노트'이자 길 찾는 이에게 띄우는
두꺼운 편지. 각 권마다 37점의 흑백
사진과 캡션이 담겼다. 인생이란 한 편의
이야기이며 '에세이'란 그 이야기를
남겨놓는 것이니. 삶의 화두와도 같은
주제로 해마다 새 시리즈가 출간된다.

136p | 20,000KRW | 2019-2020

Park Nohae Photo Essay

01 One Day
02 Simply, Firmly, Gracefully
03 The Path

These are 'wandering notes' that
the poet Park Nohae has recorded
while walking along the Earth's long,
high roads for over twenty years,
a thick letter to those who seek for
a path. Each volume contains 37
black-and-white photos and captions.
Life is a story, and each of these
'essays' is designed to leave that story
behind. A new volume is published
every year like a topic of life.

걷는 독서

단 한 줄로도 충분하다! 한 권의 책이
응축된 듯한 423편의 문장들. 박노해
시인이 감옥 독방에 갇혀서도, 국경 너머
분쟁 현장에서도 멈추지 않은 일생의
의례이자 창조의 원천인 '걷는 독서'.
온몸으로 살고 사랑하고 저항해온 삶의
정수가 담긴 문장과 세계의 숨은 빛을
담은 컬러사진이 어우러져 언제 어디를
펼쳐봐도 지혜와 영감이 깃든다.

880p | 23,000KRW | 2021

Reading While Walking Along

One line is enough! 423 sentences, one whole
book condensed into each sentence. 'Reading
While Walking Along' is a lifelong ritual and
source of creation by Park Nohae who never
stopped, even after being confined in solitary
confinement in a prison cell or at the scene of
conflicts beyond the border. The aphorisms that
contain the essence of his life, in which he has
lived, loved and resisted with his whole body,
are harmonized with color photos that contain
the hidden light of the world, delivering wisdom
and inspiration wherever we open them.

푸른 빛의 소녀가

박노해 시인의 첫 번째 시 그림책. 저 먼
행성에서 찾아온 푸른 빛의 소녀와 지구별
시인의 가슴 시린 이야기. "지구에서
좋은 게 뭐죠?" 우주적 시야로 바라본
삶의 근본 물음과 아이들의 가슴에 푸른
빛의 상상력을 불어넣는 신비로운 여정이
펼쳐진다. "우리 모두는 별에서 온 아이들.
네 안에는 별이 빛나고 있어."(박노해)

72p | 19,500KRW | 2020

The Blue Light Girl

Poet Park Nohae's first Poetry
Picture Book. The poignant tale of
the Blue Light Girl visiting from
a distant planet and a poet of Planet
Earth. "What is good on Earth?"
The fundamental question of life seen
from a cosmic perspective. A mysterious
journey inspiring an imagination of
blue light in the heart of the children.
"We are all children from the stars.
Stars are shining in you."(Park Nohae)

그러니 그대 사라지지 말아라

영혼을 뒤흔드는 시의 정수. 저항과
영성, 교육과 살림, 아름다움과 혁명
그리고 사랑까지 붉디 붉은 304편의
시가 담겼다. 인생의 갈림길에서 길을
잃고 헤매는 순간마다 어디를 펼쳐
읽어도 좋은 책. 입소문만으로 이 시집
을 구입한 6만 명의 독자가 증명하는
감동. "그러니 그대 사라지지 말아라"
그 한 마디가 나를 다시 살게 한다.

560p | 18,000KRW | 2010

So You Must Not Disappear

The essence of soul-shaking poetry!
This anthology of 304 poems as red as
its book cover, narrating resistance, spiri-
tuality, education, living, the beautiful,
revolution and love. Whenever you're lost
at a crossroads of your life, it will guide
you with any page of it moving you.
The intensity of moving is evidenced by
the 60,000 readers who have bought
this book only through word-of-mouth.
"So you must not disappear". This one
phrase makes me live again.

다른 길

"우리 인생에는 각자가 진짜로 원하는
무언가가 있다. 분명, 나만의 다른 길이
있다." 인디아에서 파키스탄, 라오스,
버마, 인도네시아, 티베트까지 지도에도
없는 마을로 떠나는 여행. 그리고 그
길의 끝에서 진정한 나를 만나는 새로운
여행에세이. '이야기가 있는 사진'이
한 걸음 다른 길로 우리를 안내한다.

352p | 19,500KRW | 2014

Another Way

"In our lives, there is something
which each of us really wants. For
me, certainly, I have my own way,
different from others"(Park Nohae).
From India, Pakistan, Laos, Burma,
Indonesia to Tibet, a journey to
villages nowhere to be seen on the
map. And a new essay of meeting
true self at the end of the road.
'Image with a story' guide us to
another way.

노동의 새벽

1984년, 27살의 '얼굴 없는 시인'이 쓴
시집 한 권이 세상을 뒤흔들었다. 독재
정부의 금서 조치에도 100만 부 이상
발간되며 화인처럼 새겨진 불멸의 고전.
억압받는 천만 노동자의 영혼의 북소리
로 울려퍼진 노래. "박노해는 역사이고
상징이며 신화다. 문학사적으로나 사회
사적으로 우리는 그런 존재를 다시 만날
수 없을지 모른다."(문학평론가 도정일)

172p | 12,000KRW | 2014
30th Anniversary Edition

The Dawn of Labor

In 1984, an anthology of poems written
by 27 years old 'faceless poet' shook Korean society. Recorded as a million seller
despite the publication ban under military
dictatorship, it became an immortal classic
ingrained like a marking iron. It was a song
echoing down with the throbbing pulses
of ten million workers' souls. "Park Nohae
is a history, a symbol, and a myth. All the
way through the history of literature and
society alike, we may never meet such a
being again."(Doh Jeong-il, literary critic)

사람만이 희망이다

34살의 나이에 '불온한 혁명가'로 무기
징역을 선고받은 박노해. 그가 1평 남짓
한 독방에 갇혀 7년 동안 써내려간 옥중
에세이. "90년대 최고의 정신적 각성"
으로 기록되는 이 책은, 희망이 보이지
않는 오늘날 더 큰 울림으로 되살아
난다. 살아있는 한 희망은 끝나지 않았
다고. 다시, 사람만이 희망이라고.

320p | 15,000KRW | 2015

Only a Person is Hope

Park Nohae was sentenced to life imprisonment as a "rebellious revolutionary"
when he was 34 years old. This essay
written in solitary confinement measu-
ring about three sq. m. for seven years.
This book is recorded as the "best
spiritual awakening in the 90s", is born
again with the bigger impression
today when there seems to be no hope
at all. As long as you live, hope never
ends. Again, only a person is hope.

단순하게 단단하게 단아하게

박노해 사진에세이 02

2판 1쇄 발행 2022년 1월 4일
초판 1쇄 발행 2020년 1월 16일

사진·글 박노해
번역 안선재
편집 김예슬, 윤지영
표지 디자인 홍동원 표제 글씨 박노해
자문 이기명 아날로그 인화 유철수
제작 윤지혜 홍보 마케팅 이상훈
인쇄 자문 유화컴퍼니 인쇄 세현인쇄
제본 광성문화사 후가공 신화사금박

발행인 임소희
발행처 느린걸음
출판등록 2002년 3월 15일 제300-2009-109호
주소 서울시 종로구 사직로8길 34, 330호
전화 02-733-3773
팩스 02-734-1976
이메일 slow-walk@slow-walk.com
홈페이지 www.slow-walk.com
instagram.com/slow_walk_book

ⓒ 박노해 2020
ISBN 978-89-91418-27-1 04810
ISBN 978-89-91418-25-7 04810(세트)

번역자 안선재(안토니 수사)는 서강대학교 명예교수로
40권 이상의 한국 시와 소설의 영문 번역서를 펴냈다.

Simply, Firmly, Gracefully

Park Nohae Photo Essay 02

Second edition, first publishing, Jan. 4, 2022
First edition, first publishing, Jan. 16, 2020

Photographed and Written by Park Nohae
Translated by Brother Anthony of Taizé
Edited by Kim Yeseul, Yun Jiyoung
Cover Designed by Hong Dongwon
Handwritten Title by Park Nohae
Consulted by Lee Ki-Myoung
Photographic Analogue Prints by Yu Chulsu
Making by Yun Jihye Marketing by Lee Sanghoon
Print Consulted by UHWACOMPANY

Publisher Im Sohee
Publishing Company Slow Walking
Address Rm330, 34, Sajik-ro 8-gil, Jongno-gu,
Seoul, Republic of Korea
Tel 82-2-7333773 Fax 82-2-7341976
E-mail slow-walk@slow-walk.com
Website www.slow-walk.com
instagram.com/slow_walk_book

ⓒ Park Nohae 2020
ISBN 978-89-91418-27-1 04810
ISBN 978-89-91418-25-7 04810(SET)

Translator An Sonjae(Brother Anthony of Taizé)
is professor emeritus at Sogang University.
He has published over forty volumes of
translations of Korean poetry and fiction.